For Mathew P – M.S.
For my family – M.H.

SIMON & SCHUSTER

First published in Great Britain in 2021 by
Simon & Schuster UK Ltd
1st Floor, 222 Gray's Inn Road, London WC1X 8HB

Text copyright © 2021 Mark Sperring
Illustrations copyright © 2021 Matt Hunt

The right of Mark Sperring & Matt Hunt to be identified as the
author and illustrator of this work has been asserted by them in
accordance with the Copyright, Designs and Patents Act, 1988

A CIP catalogue record for this book is available from the British Library upon request

PB ISBN: 978-1-4711-8448-2 ▪ eBook ISBN: 978-1-4711-8449-9
Printed in China   10 9 8 7 6 5 4 3 2 1

IF MY DAD WERE THE
TOOTH FAIRY

MARK SPERRING

MATT HUNT

IF MY DAD WERE THE TOOTH FAIRY

MARK SPERRING

MATT HUNT

SIMON & SCHUSTER

London   New York   Sydney   Toronto   New Delhi

My Dad works in an office block, which I suppose is nice,
I'm not sure what he does there, but he's told me once or twice . . .

He taps on a computer,
has a workmate who's called Bob.

Sometimes, I think, how would Dad do
in a more *high-flying* job....

If my Dad were the Tooth Fairy,
he'd work 'most every night.

He wouldn't slouch around in jeans

but wear blue spangled tights.
Wings would sprout out from his back,

he'd lift right off the ground.
And he'd be a sight to see . . .

... just fluttering around!

If my Dad were the Tooth Fairy, he'd ALWAYS be on call . . .

BEEP!

BEEP!

BEEP!

TOOTH ALERT
LATERAL
INCISOR
12 GREEN LANE

And at a moment's notice he'd go anywhere at all.

He'd grab a bag of coins

and a VERY HANDY map,

He'd snatch his wand
back from the dog,

and then his wings
would flap.

If my Dad were the Tooth Fairy,
he'd be like Mighty Man!

Except he'd have more SPARKLE
and a LOVELY diamond crown.

He'd fly out of our window
and call a quick 'goodbye!'

GOODBYE!

And then I'd watch his silhouette
go ZOOMING 'cross the sky.

If my Dad were the Tooth Fairy,
he'd be light on his feet.

CLOMP!

CLOMP!

CLOMP!

He wouldn't walk the way
he does when he CLOMPS
down the street.

He'd tiptoe up to tiny beds,
THEN, quiet as a mouse . . .

CREAK!

. . . He'd swap a tooth
for a coin, then . . .

FLITTER out the house!

But . . . if my Dad were the Tooth Fairy,
bedtime would be GRIM . . .

As he'd never really have the time for stories or tuck-ins.

He'd wander in each morning with his fairy crown askew,

Looking OH-SO-TIRED
from the night he'd just been through.

So, I'm GLAD my Dad's not the Tooth Fairy,
even though it MIGHT be funny,

But . . .

BOING,

BOING,

BOING,

imagine if . . .

. . . My Gran were

the Easter Bunny!

3 FUN FACTS ABOUT THE REAL TOOTH FAIRY

① The Tooth Fairy has no need to raid children's piggy banks – she conjures up whole piles of shiny coins with just a wave of her wand! KERCHING!

② The Tooth Fairy has never CLOMPED in her life, she flitters and flutters everywhere.

③ The Tooth Fairy thinks Dads are totally WONDERFUL but that her very UNIQUE and MAGICAL job is best done by herself! (Sorry, Dads – keep the day job!)

I've appeared three times in this book already! Did you spot me?

See me on pages 7, 14 and 16